I Like
Black and White

Barbara Jean Hicks and Lila Prap

HUTCHINSON
LONDON SYDNEY AUCKLAND JOHANNESBURG

Stinky

slinky

large

and small

woolly

short
and tall

stripes

patches

squares

and spots

lots and lots

twinkly skies

snowy lands

music

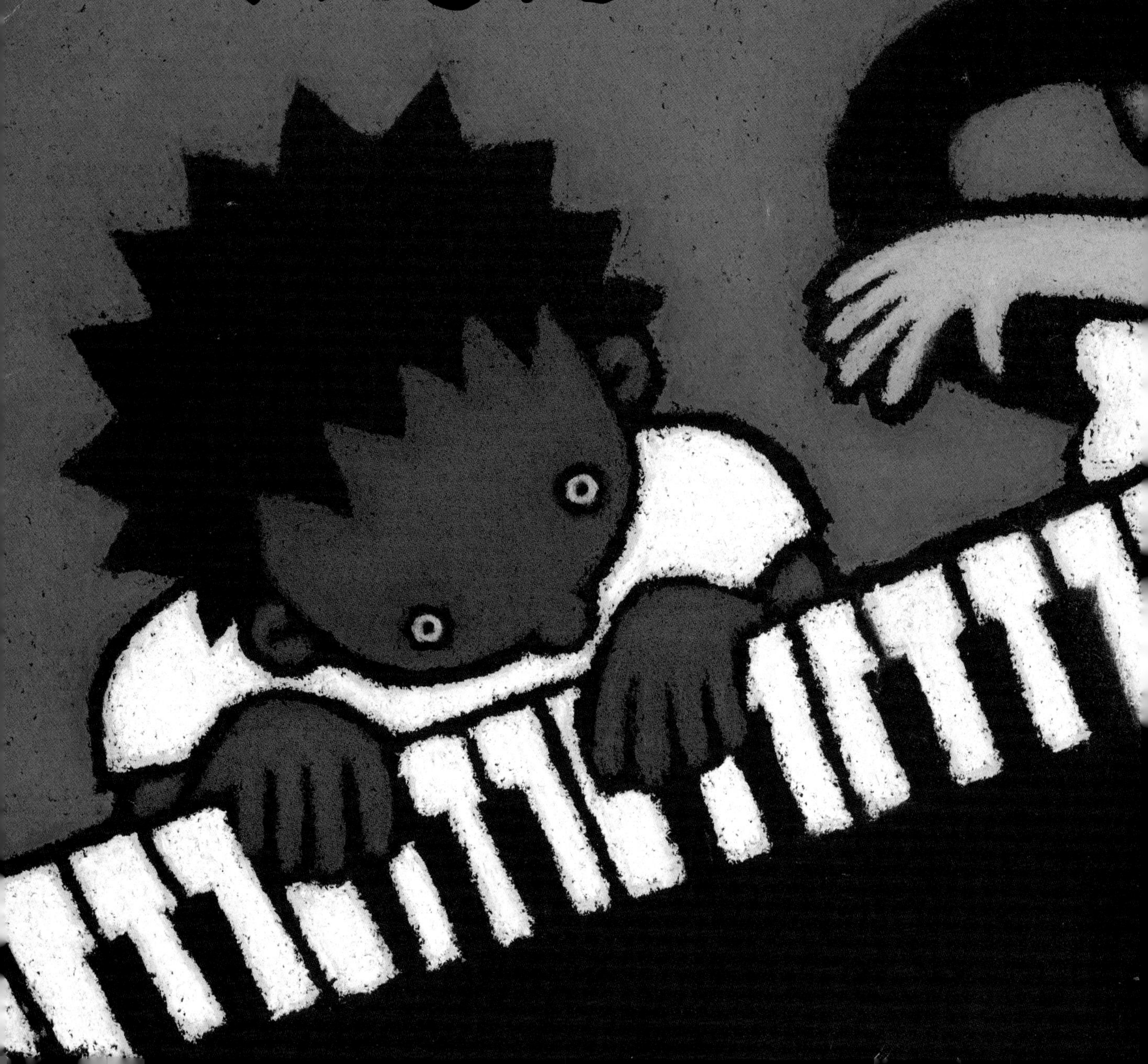

dancing

feet...

and hands!